Shipwrecked

'Shipwrecked'
An original concept by Jenny Jinks
© Jenny Jinks 2022

Illustrated by Laura Deo

Published by MAVERICK ARTS PUBLISHING LTD
Studio 11, City Business Centre, 6 Brighton Road,
Horsham, West Sussex, RH13 5BB
© Maverick Arts Publishing Limited August 2022
+44 (0)1403 256941

A CIP catalogue record for this book is available at the British Library.

ISBN 978-1-84886-897-7

Maverick publishing
www.maverickbooks.co.uk

Green

This book is rated as: Green Band (Guided Reading)
It follows the requirements for Phase 5 phonics.
Most words are decodable, and any non-decodable words are familiar, supported by the context and/or represented in the artwork.

Shipwrecked

By Jenny Jinks

Illustrated by Laura Deo

Prem was in her spaceship when, all of a sudden... WHOOSH! A big space rock came and...

...CRASH!

It smashed into Prem's ship!

Prem crashed onto a new planet.

Her ship was broken. It did not start.

Prem was scared and all alone.

Prem was shipwrecked!

Prem wrote a message home.

'Help! I am stuck on a little red planet. Prem.'

She pressed a button and sent it.

Prem waited to be rescued.

But nobody came.

Prem was hungry and tired.

Then, Prem saw something move.

Prem was scared. She was not alone.

Nak crept up to Prem.

"Gup?" said Nak. He gave her a blue fruit.

Prem bit into the fruit. It was yummy!

The next day, Nak gave Prem more food.

Prem ate it all. But the gup fruit was the best.

Prem showed Nak how to play with a ball.

Nak loved playing catch.

Nak took Prem to his home,

so she could meet Nak's family.

They let Prem stay with them.

Prem loved Nak and the little red planet.

But she missed her own family.

One day, Prem heard a noise.

Prem and Nak went to see.

It was a ship.

"Look!" said Prem. "It's my family!"

Prem wanted her family to meet Nak.

But Nak was hiding. He was scared.

Prem went to find Nak.

"I have to go home now," said Prem.

She said goodbye to Nak and his family.

Nak gave Prem a gup fruit to take with her.

Prem got on the ship and her family hugged her.

As they blasted off, Prem looked out of the window.

Nak was waving. Prem waved back.

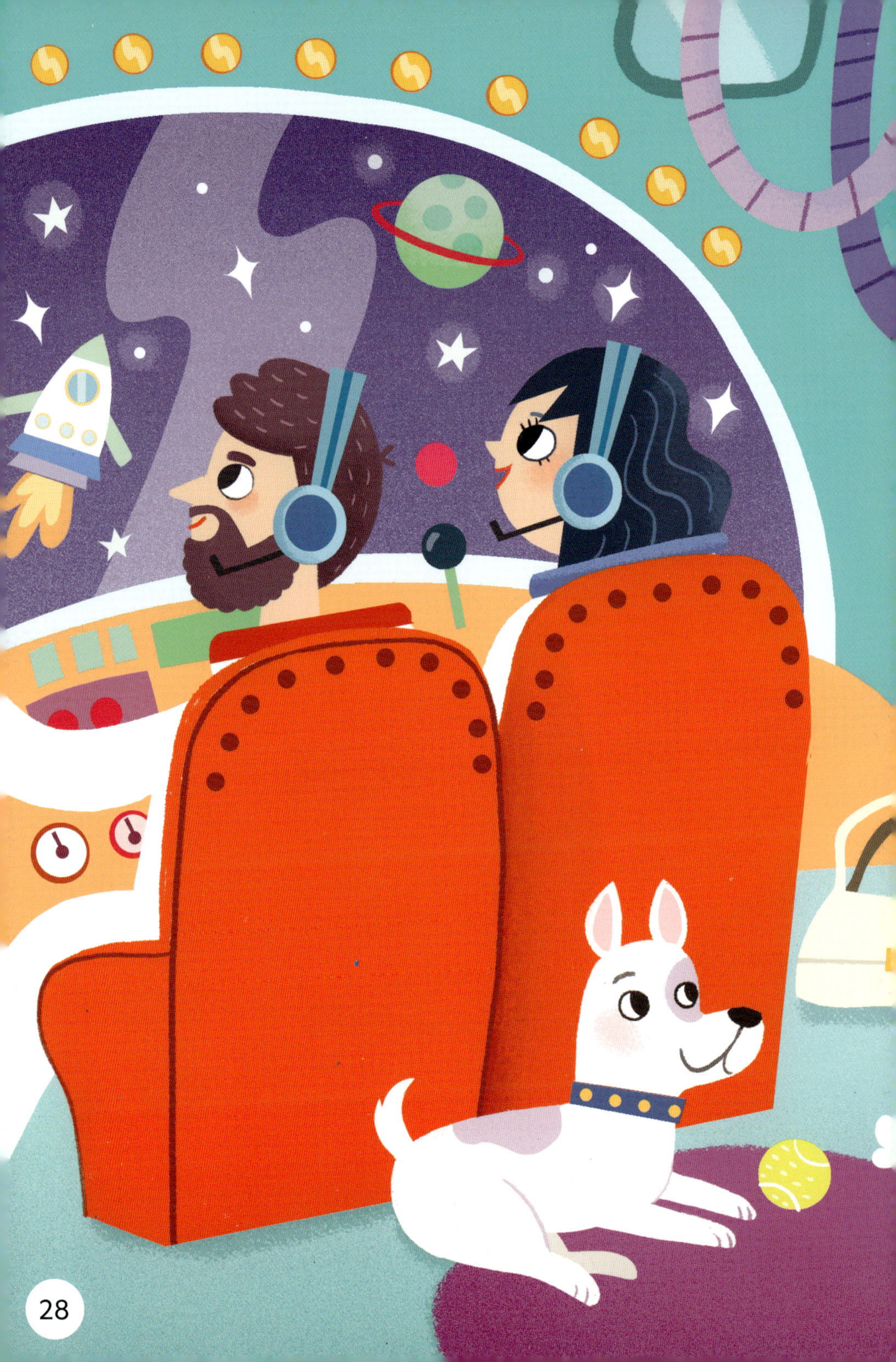

Prem missed Nak and the red planet.

But she would visit him again.

Until then, Nak would be her secret.

Quiz

1. Where does Prem crash?
a) A big blue planet
b) A small yellow planet
c) A little red planet

2. What blue fruit does Nak give Prem?
a) Gup
b) Bub
c) Pop

3. What did Prem show Nak?
a) How to play ball
b) How to steer a ship
c) How to play tag

4. Why did Nak hide from Prem's family?
a) He was playing hide and seek
b) He was scared
c) He wanted to surprise them

5. What did Prem and Nak do as the ship blasted off?
a) They waved
b) They danced
c) They jumped

Turn over for answers

Book Bands for Guided Reading

The Institute of Education book banding system is a scale of colours that reflects the various levels of reading difficulty. The bands are assigned by taking into account the content, the language style, the layout and phonics. Word, phrase and sentence level work is also taken into consideration.

Maverick Early Readers are a bright, attractive range of books covering the pink to white bands. All of these books have been book banded for guided reading to the industry standard and edited by a leading educational consultant.

Pink
Red
Yellow
Blue
Green
Orange
Turquoise
Purple
Gold
White

To view the whole Maverick Readers scheme, visit our website at www.maverickearlyreaders.com

Or scan the QR code above to view our scheme instantly!

Quiz Answers: 1c, 2a, 3a, 4b, 5a